The Vactooine Disaster

This galaxy is yours.
Be a part of

#1 Assault on Yavin Four

#2 Escape from Thyferra

#3 Attack on Delrakkin

#4 Destroy the Liquidator

#5 The Hunt for Han Solo

#6 The Search for Grubba the Hutt

#7 Ithorian Invasion

#8 Togorian Trap

#9 Revolt of the Battle Droids

#10 Showdown in Mos Eisley

#11 Bounty Hunters vs. Battle Droids

#12 The Vactooine Disaster

. . . and more to come!

#12

The Vactooine Disaster

RYDER WINDHAM

SCHOLASTIC INC.
New York Toronto London Auckland Sydney

ISBN 0-590-59269-6

12 11 10 9 8 7 6 5 4 3 2 1 8 9/9 0 1 2 3/0

Printed in the U.S.A.

First Scholastic printing, August 1998

The Vactooine Disaster

INTRODUCTION

After an army of renegade droids attempted to attack Jabba the Hutt's palace on the desert planet Tatooine, Jabba hired bounty hunters to pursue the droids and capture their drone barge. One bounty hunter succeeded in this mission, tracking the droids to the Vactooine system and bringing their drone barge back to Tatooine.

During his mission, the bounty hunter learned that the automatons had stolen the Victory Star Destroyer *Decimator* from the Empire. They had used *Decimator* to transport the drone barge to the Vactooine system. The bounty hunter also learned the renegades had little interest in Jabba, that in fact the evil droid EV-9D9 had been their target in Jabba's palace.

On Vactooine, the automatons easily defeated the mining colonists. The droids rounded up the miners, intending to use them to build a droid manufacturing factory.

When the Rebels on Yavin Four did not receive a shipment of metals from Vactooine, Luke Skywalker feared that Vactooine's mining colony might have been conquered by the Empire. Without knowing about the renegade droids, the Rebels raced to Vactooine, unprepared for the danger that awaited them. . . .

Preliminary Mission

CHAPTER ONE

Tatooine's twin suns were rising over the vast horizon as Jabba the Hutt examined the immense drone barge, stolen from the renegade droids. The barge rested on a rocky plateau, not far from the Hutt's palace.

At first, Jabba had been greatly disappointed that there were no droids on the barge. He could have used the droids or sold them for a profit. Not wanting to pay for an empty barge, Jabba had protested to the bounty hunter who had retrieved the vessel from the Vactooine system. But the bounty hunter had reminded Jabba that his order had been to bring the barge back to Tatooine, with or without any droids. The bounty hunter had also pointed out that the barge was in good shape, considering it had been through a couple of battles. Realizing the barge was valuable, Jabba paid the bounty hunter.

The bounty hunter also informed Jabba that the droids had taken over a Victory Star Destroyer named *Decimator*. Jabba considered contacting the Empire to tell them he had information about *Decimator*, but he did not enjoy dealing with Imperials. He was also concerned that the drone barge might have been Imperial property. Now that he had paid money for the barge, Jabba was determined to keep it.

Jabba sent his chief lieutenant Bib Fortuna to inspect the interior of the ship. An hour later, Fortuna stepped out of the barge, descending the ramp to the rocky ground where Jabba waited. Jabba was lounging on his floating dais, munching on some bite-sized lizards. Fortuna approached the Hutt with caution, frightened of interrupting Jabba during a meal.

His mouth full of squirming snacks, Jabba mumbled, “Is the barge's interior in good condition?”

“Yes, mighty Jabba,” Fortuna replied, adjusting his long head tails around his shoulders. “There is minor damage to some of the equipment. Shall I have your maintenance droids make the necessary repairs?”

“No!” Jabba answered with a sputter. The bounty hunter had also told Jabba that the renegade automatons had wanted to destroy EV-9D9, who controlled the droid operations in Jabba's palace. Although the Hutt was glad to know the droids were not trying to kill him, he was also insulted. It seemed to him that the renegades thought EV-9D9 was more *important* than he was. Jabba would never allow EV-9D9 to believe the same thing.

“No,” Jabba repeated, gulping down the last of the lizards. “The renegade automatons might have contaminated the barge for other droids. I want Barada to make any repairs. Tell him to wipe the memory banks of the drone barge's computers.” Barada was one of the most hardworking creatures in Jabba's palace, maintaining all the Hutt's vehicles.

“Yes, mighty Jabba,” Fortuna replied. “I will summon Barada at once.”

“One more thing,” Jabba added. “I don't think the droids *bought* this ship from anyone. Before Barada erases all the memory banks, tell him I want to know who owned this barge before the automatons obtained it.”

An expression of great concern crossed Bib Fortuna's

face. "I . . . forgive me, master, but I thought you already knew!"

"Knew what?" Jabba demanded. "Spit it out, Fortuna!"

Gaping, Bib Fortuna turned and pointed to the side of the barge's ramp, where a small metal panel was bolted in place. The metal panel was a sign, containing information written in both Basic and Huttese. Jabba narrowed his large eyes, carefully reading the small sign.

"*'Property of Boonda the Hutt',*" Jabba read aloud. "Boonda the droid manufacturer? Well, I'll be farkled!"

Standing by the ruins of his droid factory, Boonda the Hutt and an Imperial soldier watched the *Lambda*-class shuttle rise up and away from Boonda's Moon, the third moon in the Kleeva system. The Empire had responded to Admiral Groot's distress beacon, sending the Lambda shuttle to rescue Groot and Captain Pelvin. The Imperial soldier had remained on Boonda's Moon to keep an eye on Boonda. The shuttle rose quickly, soon becoming a distant, vanishing dot in the sky.

The Imperial soldier had fought bravely against the renegade droids, and Boonda did not mind the soldier's company. If not for the soldier, Boonda would have been without allies on his own moon.

"I'm going to check on some supplies, Boonda," the Imperial soldier stated. "I'll also see if I can salvage anything from the wreckage." The soldier walked off toward the factory ruins.

Despite the evidence, Boonda could not believe his droids were capable of such violence — slaying his partner

Olag Greck in cold blood and attacking the crew of the Star Destroyer *Decimator*. Casting a glance across the remains of his factory, Boonda realized he might never find poor Olag's body.

Boonda had no idea where the droids might have gone, but he feared they were surely causing more trouble somewhere in the galaxy. The Hutt had promised Admiral Groot that he would contact the Empire if he learned of the droids' whereabouts.

Since all of Boonda's communications equipment had been destroyed during the droids' attack, the Lambda shuttle had delivered a powerful HoloNet comm unit to Boonda's Moon. With this device, Boonda could send and receive messages over the HoloNet, the intergalactic communications system controlled by the Empire. The HoloNet used transceivers routed through hyperspace, allowing for nearly instant communication between distant planets. If Boonda were to learn anything about his renegade droids, he could notify Admiral Groot immediately.

Boonda was surprised when a light began flashing on the comm unit, indicating that someone was trying to contact him.

"Who could be trying to call me now?" Boonda wondered aloud. After all, Admiral Groot had only just left.

A green light flared from the comm unit, generating a holographic image of the caller. The hologram shifted to face Boonda, who recognized the caller immediately. It was the vile gangster Jabba the Hutt.

"Well, hello, Jabba," Boonda said without any surprise in his voice. "To what do I owe this pleasure?"

"Tell me something, Boonda," Jabba's hologram muttered, ignoring Boonda's greeting. "How do you happen to have an Imperial HoloNet comm unit?"

"It was a gift from an admiral," Boonda declared, telling the truth. "You appear to possess an Imperial comm unit too, Jabba. How did you get yours?"

Jabba's hologram chuckled. "I stole it, of course," he answered. "So, I figured *if* you were still alive, the Empire would have supplied you with a HoloNet comm. After everything that's happened, Boonda, I suppose the Imperial Navy wants to keep track of you!"

"Whatever do you mean?" Boonda asked, realizing that Jabba was toying with him. "Do you think I'm in some sort of trouble with the Empire?"

"That depends," Jabba answered mysteriously. "Did the admiral give you the comm unit before or after your droids captured *Decimator*?"

Boonda forced himself to grin. He did not know how Jabba had found out about the droids, but he would not let Jabba take advantage of him. "Really, Jabba!" Boonda sighed. "Can't an Imperial officer just give me a present because he *likes* me?"

"Somehow, I don't think so," Jabba's hologram answered, narrowing his gaze on Boonda. "But what I *do* think is that you and I might have some *business* to discuss. You see, my palace came under attack by an army of droids, flying in an old drone barge. The barge belonged to you, so I know the droids came from your factory. I know you would never have *deliberately* released malfunctioning droids, Boonda."

Taking a quick glance toward the factory ruins, Boonda noted that the Imperial soldier was not within sight. Boonda turned back to Jabba's hologram, wondering what the other Hutt had in mind. "You had better not be attempting to blackmail me, Jabba!"

"Me? Blackmail? Pshaw!" Jabba replied. "I already told you, this is a matter of *business*. I'm sure the Empire wants their Star Destroyer back. I have learned the location of *Decimator* and your renegade droids. Your admiral would appreciate it if you were to give him this information. Just keep my name out of it. I don't want any trouble from the Empire."

"What exactly *do* you want, Jabba?" Boonda inquired.

Jabba's hologram grinned. "I forgot to mention that your drone barge is now parked outside my palace," the gangster leered. "There weren't any droids on board, but it's a fine, sturdy ship. I will give you the location of *Decimator* if you will allow me to keep your barge."

Boonda was impressed. Jabba had actually presented a decent deal. If Boonda could help Admiral Groot recover *Decimator* and stop the renegade automatons, it might stop the droids from harming anyone else.

"Deal!" Boonda agreed. Jabba gave *Decimator*'s location to Boonda. When their conversation was over, Boonda switched the comm unit off.

Resetting the HoloNet comm unit, Boonda punched in a sequence of keys. Seconds later, Admiral Groot's hologram appeared from the comm.

"What is it, Boonda?" Groot's hologram demanded. "We were just about to enter hyperspace! Have you heard something about the escaped droids?"

"Yes, Admiral," Boonda answered. In order to keep Jabba's name out of the story, Boonda would have to lie a little. Unlike other Hutts, Boonda did not enjoy lying very much. Taking a deep breath, the Hutt proclaimed, "An old friend told me he saw my drone barge in the Vactooine system!"

CHAPTER TWO

Admiral Groot turned off the holo comm unit in the Lambda shuttle. Groot didn't know what to do next. The Lambda shuttle carried twenty troops, but he did not want to call for any Imperial reinforcements without knowing the precise location of *Decimator*.

Turning to Captain Pelvin, Admiral Groot declared, "We should set course for Vactooine right away. If we find *Decimator* there, we'll contact Imperial City to send reinforcements."

Captain Pelvin had witnessed Groot's conversation with the Hutt. "Forgive me, Admiral, but there's something odd about the Hutt's message."

"What do you mean?" Admiral Groot asked. "You can't still be thinking Boonda is trying to trick us. He helped blow up his own factory while trying to stop the renegade droids!"

"I agree, Admiral, but it seems strange that Boonda would learn this new information so soon. His message came almost immediately after he thought we were safely off his moon. I've also never known a Hutt who had any *real* friends!"

"Boonda's timing does seem a bit too fast," Groot admitted. "And you're right about Hutts not having friends. Do you suspect this is some sort of elaborate trap?"

"I don't know, Admiral," Pelvin replied. "But it might be to our advantage to bring Boonda *with* us to the Vactooine system."

Admiral Groot nodded. "That's not a bad idea," he commented. Groot leaned forward in his seat, ordering the Lambda shuttle's pilot to fly back to Boonda's Moon. The shuttle banked hard, returning to the third moon in the Kleeva system.

"We'll bring Boonda along for the ride to Vactooine," Groot declared. "If we find any trace of *Decimator*, his droids or barge, we'll owe him our thanks and an apology."

As the Lambda descended upon Boonda's Moon, Pelvin asked, "And what if Boonda is lying?"

"If he's lying," Groot muttered through clenched teeth, "the Hutt will die by inches!"

Minutes after the Imperials had unexpectedly returned to his moon, Boonda the Hutt found himself squeezed into the back of their *Lambda*-class shuttle. Admiral Groot had told him they wanted Boonda to introduce them to his friend in the Vactooine system.

"But, my friend might not *be* there anymore," Boonda had answered. "He only said he *sighted* my drone barge. He didn't say he would stay and keep an eye on it. I merely passed the information on to you. I need to stay here — what if he tries to contact me again?"

Groot had ordered an Imperial soldier to remain on Boonda's Moon and monitor the HoloNet comm unit. The admiral had then insisted Boonda join them. The Hutt had not been in any position to argue.

Including Groot and Pelvin, there were twenty troops on board the Lambda shuttle. Because of his size, Boonda was forced to sit beside a landspeeder on the floor of the cargo bay. The floor was cold and uncomfortable but Boonda offered no complaints to the ten heavily armed stormtroopers who sat facing him from their seats.

The Hutt closed his eyes, pretending to fall asleep. His mind was racing, trying to figure out how he was going to get himself out of this mess. He had told Admiral Groot that the drone barge was in the Vactooine system, knowing it was really on Tatooine. Boonda knew better than to tell Admiral Groot about the deal with Jabba. If Groot did not kill Boonda for lying, Jabba would kill Boonda for telling the truth.

Suddenly, the Lambda shuttle's engines roared as the ship entered hyperspace. Boonda shuddered slightly, feeling his stomach churn at the very thought of hyperspace travel.

The Hutt opened his eyes, letting his gaze travel to a bright red switch built into the wall at his left. Boonda wondered if he could reach the switch without being shot by the stormtroopers. He would probably only have one chance, and he would have to wait until the Lambda shuttle had exited hyperspace.

Realizing the game was not yet over, Boonda smiled. The Hutt was glad he had been placed in the cargo bay.

The red switch was for the emergency escape pod.

CHAPTER THREE

The Star Destroyer *Decimator* had landed beside the mining colony spaceport on the planet Vactooine. The traffic controller droid Wuntoo Forcee Forwun stood outside *Decimator*, surveying the colony's dozen modular buildings.

Since the miners possessed few weapons, it had been an easy victory for the droids. The human and alien colonists had been rounded up and placed within a warehouse building. Soon the miners would be put to work, following the droids' orders to build a new droid manufacturing facility.

But the voyage to Vactooine had not been easy for the renegade automatons. Although the droids had escaped Boonda's Moon and taken over the Star Destroyer *Decimator*, a number of droids had been destroyed by aliens on Tatooine. Even more droids had been demolished in the Vactooine system when a lone spacer had attacked the *Decimator* and stolen Boonda's drone barge.

Forwun walked to the edge of a plastoid landing platform where the personal attendant droids BP-A1 and BP-A2 hovered over several pieces of mangled metal. The pieces were the remains of the chef droid K-2PQ.

"Can you fix him?" Forwun asked the two attendant droids.

"We hope so," replied BP-A1.

"We can only try," added BP-A2 as he used a hydrospanner to open K-2PQ's metal skull. "We don't blame you, Forwun."

"Blame me for what?" Forwun inquired, puzzled by the floating droid's comment.

"Well, we know how much you wanted to get EV-9D9," BP-A1 stated, referring to the evil droid who had destroyed so many of Forwun's fellow 1-2 units in the Bespin system. "If we had just come straight to Vactooine instead of trying to find EV-9D9 on Tatooine, we might not have lost so many droids."

"And K-2PQ might still be in one piece," BP-A2 added, making another adjustment to the chef droid's circuits.

Forwun did not know what to say, so he walked away from the attendant droids. Forwun knew BP-A1 and BP-A2 were right. The traffic controller droid would not rest until EV-9D9 was reduced to scrap metal, but he had taken an unnecessary risk on Tatooine. Lost in thought, Forwun approached the *Decimator* to oversee the dozens of droids who were busily salvaging Imperial equipment.

"Psssst!" a voice hissed from the doorway of a spaceport office. Forwun spun fast, turning to see a dark hooded figure standing beside a Gamorrean guard.

Drawing and raising his blaster at the mysterious pair, Forwun exclaimed, "Surrender at once!"

Pulling back his cloak, the hooded figure revealed himself to be an alien with reptilian skin. He had long, pointed ears on his hairless head and a small mouth filled with sharp teeth. In response to Forwun, the alien commanded, "Voice Override: Epsilon Actual. Password: *Takeover*!"

The alien's words had a strange effect on Forwun, causing a flutter in the droid's cogitative theory unit. The droid's arm lowered to his side, aiming the blaster at the ground.

"You're late, Forwun," the alien said. "I expected the *Decimator* to arrive yesterday."

"Sorry about the blaster, sir. I didn't recognize you at first." The alien was Forwun's master and the Gamorrean was the alien's personal bodyguard. Forwun felt confused, wondering how he could have forgotten his own master.

"No harm done," said the reptilian alien. "But what delayed your journey to Vactooine?"

"We were detained on Tatooine, sir," Forwun answered.

"Tatooine!" the reptilian alien snapped. "Tatooine wasn't part of my plan!" Stepping forward, he removed the blaster from Forwun's hand, then gave the droid a sharp rap on the skull. "You were supposed to come straight here from Boonda's Moon!"

"Sorry, sir," Forwun answered. The droid was very confused by the sight of the alien. For some reason, Forwun had thought his master was dead. The droid realized something must have happened to his memory banks. Looking at his surroundings, Forwun became even more bewildered. "May I ask a question?"

"By all means," the reptilian alien encouraged.

"What planet are we on, Master Greck?"

After leaving the Rebel's secret base on Yavin Four, the *Millennium Falcon* and four X-wings from Rogue Squadron blasted into hyperspace. The ships flew together in a tight formation, speeding toward the Vactooine system.

In the *Falcon*'s cockpit, Han Solo and Chewbacca the Wookiee were at the controls, with Princess Leia Organa and Luke Skywalker seated behind them. See-Threepio, Artoo-Detoo, and Q-7N were strapped into the *Falcon*'s main hold area.

The *Falcon*'s cockpit was illuminated by the bizarre cascade of hyperspace. Solo and Chewbacca squinted their eyes as they adjusted the controls.

"I hope Wedge Antilles and the other pilots are keeping up with us," Leia said.

"I'm sure they're doing fine," Solo observed. Turning to Luke, Solo commented, "I hope you're wrong about any problems on Vactooine, kid."

"Me too, Han," Luke replied. "But when the shipment of Vactooine metal didn't arrive on Yavin Four, I suddenly felt that something was wrong."

Chewbacca growled a warning to Solo. "Okay," Solo replied. "Everyone tighten your belts. We're entering the Vactooine system!"

The *Millennium Falcon* and the four X-wings tore out of hyperspace, entering real space and sighting the planet Vactooine. Suddenly, an alarm began to blare from the *Falcon*'s console.

"What is it?" Leia asked.

"Our sensors have detected another ship in the area!" Solo shouted over the alarm. "It's an Imperial *Lambda*-class cruiser. Stang! I think it's spotted us!" Punching the *Falcon*'s comm unit, Solo warned Wedge and the other pilots.

"Then I was right!" Luke yelled. "There *is* Imperial activity on Vactooine. The Empire has probably taken over Vactooine's mining colony."

"We don't know that for sure, Luke," Leia retorted. "The Lambda might just be a scout ship. The only way to find out is to engage the Lambda, then investigate Vactooine."

"Whatever we do, we'd better do it fast!" Solo shouted, gripping the controls. "That Lambda is coming right at us. Everyone to their battle stations!"

Mission Briefing

Before you proceed, you must consult the Mission Guide for the rules of the STAR WARS MISSIONS. You must follow these rules at all times.

This is a Rebel mission.

You are a soldier for the Rebel Alliance. Believing there might be trouble in the Vactooine system, you have traveled to Vactooine to investigate. Exiting hyperspace, you immediately encounter an Imperial *Lambda*-class shuttle.

The Rebel Alliance is depending on a shipment of Vactooine metal for starship building and repairs. It is possible the Lambda is the only Imperial ship in the area, but you will have to explore the planet Vactooine to make certain. If the mining colony has been taken over by hostile forces, you must do everything you can to defeat the enemy and rescue the colonists.

Your goal is to discover what has caused the delay in the metal shipment. If something has happened to the mining colony, you must rescue the miners. Although you suspect the Empire is responsible, you may be up against a different enemy.

You start the mission with your MP total from your previous Mission. (If this is your first Mission, you start with 1000 MP.)

Choose your character. You can take no more than four weapons (including a blaster rifle and a laser pistol), three vehicles (one must be for space travel and another for land). You can use Power three times in this Mission.

May the Force be with you.

Your Mission: The Vactooine Disaster

Even though the Imperial Lambda shuttle is outnumbered by the Rebel ships, the shuttle turns to attack. Suddenly, the Lambda fires a concussion missile.

The missile streaks toward the Rebel vehicles. Having just emerged from hyperspace, your vehicle's weapons systems are not yet fully powered up.

To survive the Lambda's attack, choose to evade the concussion missile, with or without Power.

Choose your vehicle now (it must be capable of space travel).

To evade the Lambda's concussion missile (using Power)*: Choose your Vehicle Evasion Power. Your Power's low-resist# + your Jedi# + 1 is your confront#. Roll the 6-dice to propel your vehicle out of firing range.

> *If your confront# is equal to or more than your roll#,* add the difference +3 to your MP total. The Lambda's deadly missile speeds past your viewport, barely missing your vehicle. You may now proceed.
>
> *If your confront# is less than your roll#,* subtract the difference from your MP total. The Lambda's sudden attack startles you, leaving you unprepared. You must now transfer all your vehicle's energy to your particle shields (below).

Note: This counts as one of three Power uses you are allowed on this Mission.

To evade the Lambda's concussion missile (without Power): Your skill# + your vehicle's stealth# +5 is your confront#. Roll the 12-dice to dodge the missile.

If your confront# is equal to or more than your roll#, add the difference +5 to your MP total. The missile barely misses your vehicle. You may proceed.

If your confront# is less than your roll#, subtract the difference from your MP total. The Lambda's sudden attack startles you, leaving you unprepared. You must transfer all your vehicle's energy to your particle shields (below).

To transfer energy to your particle shields: Your skill# + your vehicle's stealth# +4 is your confront#. While your vehicle's weapons charge, roll the 12-dice to redirect energy from the vehicle's engines to your particle shields.

If your confront# is equal to or more than your roll#, add the difference to your MP total. Your particle shields surge with energy, effectively deflecting the blast of the Lambda's missile. You may now proceed.

If your confront# is less than your roll#, subtract the difference from your MP total. Repeat this confront until you have raised your fully energized particle shields, then proceed.

The Lambda's missile explodes, causing a massive shock wave. Your fully energized particle shields protect you from the blast, but the shock wave hits the other Rebel ships hard, rendering them temporarily without power. The Imperial vessel veers away from the area as your vehicle's weapons systems go on line.

Over your comm unit, your Rebel commander shouts,

"It'll take almost an hour for our vehicles to recharge. Disable the Lambda if you can! I want those Imperials alive for questioning — just prevent them from contacting the Empire!"

"Yes, sir!" you answer into your comm. Rerouting shield energy back to your engines, you head for the fleeing Imperial shuttle. Throwing the control hard to the left, you pull into a dive that gives you a clear shot at the Lambda.

Located on the Lambda's bottom hull, a communications grid contains sensors and a powerful antenna. If the Lambda transmits a HoloNet message to the Empire, more Imperial ships may invade the Vactooine system. You cannot let this happen.

The Lambda's communications grid is protected by its own powerful deflector shield. You might not be able to destroy the shield generator, but you should be able to disable it long enough to destroy the communications grid.

If you're lucky, you might be able to punch out the deflector shield and destroy the communications grid with a single blast. Your other option is to assault the Lambda in two stages, first disabling the Lambda's shield generator, then destroying its communications grid.

Choose to knock out the Lambda's shields and communications grid in a single blast or to first disable the Lambda's shield generator.

To knock out the Lambda's shield and communications grid in a single blast: Your skill# + your weaponry# + your vehicle's weaponry# +3 is your confront#. Roll the 12-dice to fire upon the Lambda's lower hull.

If your confront# is equal to or more than your roll#, add the difference + 7 to your MP total. A brilliant electric explosion erupts below the Lambda as its shield generator explodes, rupturing the communications grid. You may now proceed.

If your confront# is less than your roll#, subtract the difference from your MP total. Your targeting computer was not adjusted properly and the blast deflected off the Lambda's shield. You must now proceed to disable the Lambda's shield generator (below).

To disable the Lambda's shield generator: If you have already tried to knock out the Lambda's shield and communications grid with a single blast, your weaponry# + your vehicle's weaponry# +3 is your confront#. If this is your first shot, your weaponry# + your vehicle's weaponry# +5 is your confront#. Roll the 12-dice to fire a blast that will disable the Lambda's lower deflector shields.

If your confront# is equal to or more than your roll#, add the difference +4 to your MP total. A brilliant electric explosion erupts below the Lambda as its shield generator is knocked out. You may now proceed to destroy the Lambda's communications grid (below).

If your confront# is less than your roll#, subtract the difference from your MP total. Repeat this confront until you have knocked out the Lambda's shield generator. After the shields are down, proceed to destroy the Lambda's communications grid (below).

To destroy the Lambda's communications grid: Your vehicle's weaponry# + your weaponry# is your confront#. Roll the 6-dice to fire a blast that will disable the Lambda's ability to send and receive messages on the HoloNet.

If your confront# is equal to or more than your roll#, add the difference to your MP total. The Lambda's transmission antennae explodes in a shower of flying sparks and you may proceed.

If your confront# is less than your roll#, subtract the difference from your MP total. You missed the target and the Lambda was able to reactivate its deflector shields! You must go back to disable the Lambda's shield generator (above). After you disable the shield generator, proceed to destroy the Lambda's communications grid. Repeat the confront until you have destroyed the Lambda's communications grid, then you may proceed.

You have disabled the Lambda's ability to summon other Imperial ships. Add 20 MP to your MP total.

The Lambda shuttle rocks away from the blast, shuddering from the damage to its lower hull. Much to your amazement, an emergency escape pod blasts away from the side of the Lambda. It seems unlikely that an Imperial soldier would bail out of a fight so soon. The escape pod tumbles through space toward the planet Vactooine.

The Lambda suddenly pulls into a tight turn, angling back to attack the escape pod. As the Lambda fires a missile at the escape pod, you immediately realize the pod may contain an enemy of the Empire.

For all you know, a captured Rebel might be in the pod, making a daring escape from the Lambda. Trusting your instincts, you must destroy the Lambda's proton torpedo before it strikes the escape pod.

To destroy the Lambda's missile: Add your weaponry# to your vehicle's weaponry# for your confront#. Roll the 6-dice to fire at the proton torpedo.

> *If your confront# is equal to or more than your roll#,* add the difference to your MP total. Scoring a direct hit, the proton torpedo detonates, causing a massive explosion that stops just short of the escape pod. You may now proceed.
>
> *If your confront# is less than your roll#,* subtract the difference from your MP total. Instead of detonating the torpedo, your blast has knocked it off course, sending it hurtling toward a Rebel X-wing. Add +5 to your confront# for your new confront#. Roll the 12-dice to blast the torpedo before it strikes the X-wing.
>
> > *If your new confront# is equal to or more than your roll#,* add the difference to your MP total. The Lambda's torpedo is destroyed and you may now proceed.
> >
> > *If your new confront# is less than your roll#,* subtract 20 MP from your MP total. The torpedo hits the X-wing, and both explode in a cataclysmic fireball.

The explosion rocks the Lambda and the escape pod, sending both vessels out of control. The pod tumbles faster through space, spinning wildly toward Vactooine's stratosphere. The Lambda appears to be flying blind, on a collision course with your vehicle.

Before you can react, the Lambda's port wing smashes into the underside of your vehicle, damaging your engines and landing gear. Your console flares and smoke begins to fill the cockpit. Looking out the viewport, you see the Lambda falling toward Vactooine.

Taking a quick glance at your sensors, you notice the other Rebel vehicles are still disabled. "My ship is heavily damaged!" you announce into your comm.

"Try landing on Vactooine!" the Rebel commander answers. "Find out who's in the escape pod, and stay clear of the Lambda crew. We'll rejoin you as soon as possible!"

Trailing fire and smoke, you angle your vehicle down through Vactooine's stratosphere. As you soar through the clouds, you lose sight of the Lambda. Keeping your sensors trained on the escape pod, you try following the pod as you plummet toward a tree-covered mountaintop.

If you set your vehicle's nav computer on autopilot, you can eject, but you might get tangled in the trees. Your battle with the Lambda has damaged your vehicle's landing gear, but you are a skilled pilot and should be able to bring your ship down. Either way, you are in for a rough landing.

Choose to eject from your vehicle or to make an emergency landing.

To eject from your vehicle: Add your vehicle's stealth# to your skill# for your confront#. Roll the 6-dice to pop the canopy and launch the ejector seat.

If your confront# is equal to or more than your roll#, add the difference to your MP total. Launching away from your vehicle, you paraglide through the towering trees. Your chutes snare in some upper branches but you land safely on the ground. Flying on autopilot, your vehicle crashes through the treetops before it lands sideways on a grassy slope. You may now proceed.

If your confront# is less than your roll#, subtract the difference from your MP total. Your vehicle's canopy does not pop open, halting the ejection system. Add your strength# +3 to your confront# for your new confront#. Roll the 12-dice to push the canopy open.

If your confront# is equal to or more than your roll#, add the difference to your MP total. The canopy pops open and you rocket out of the cockpit to safety. Your vehicle lands on autopilot in the distance. You may proceed.

If your confront# is less than your roll#, subtract the difference from your MP total. The canopy resists your push, indicating the emergency ejection system is damaged beyond repair. Proceed to make an emergency landing (below).

To make an emergency landing: Add your vehicle's stealth# to your skill# +1 for your confront#. Roll the 6-dice to skim the treetops, heading for a visible clearing.

If your confront# is equal to or more than your roll#, add the difference to your MP total. Ploughing through the treetops, you maneuver your vehicle toward a grassy slope. The vehicle skids to a shuddering stop and you may proceed.

If your confront# is less than your roll#, subtract the difference from your MP total. The vehicle crashes into the ground. You are thrown from your seat as metal twists around you. Roll the 6-dice to assess the damage.

If you roll 1 or 2: Your vehicle will need serious repair. Luckily, you escape without injury.

If you roll 3 or 4: Your weapon arm is jammed when you crash. Subtract 1 from your weaponry# for the rest of this Mission.

If you roll 5 or 6: You hit your head badly in the crash. Subtract 1 from your skill# for the rest of this Mission.

Surveying your surroundings, you find you have landed in a wooded area thick with trees. From what you can see, Vactooine is a strangely beautiful planet with crimson trees and bright red grass. Gazing to the west from your position in the hills, you see what appears to be a more rocky landscape.

Inspecting your crashed vehicle, you are glad to learn it has not been damaged beyond repair. The engines and landing gear will require special parts and tools, but at least the Rebel fleet has not lost a valuable vehicle. You remove your weapons and data pad from the vessel, and prepare to set off on foot.

Remembering your commander's orders, you attempt to locate the escape pod. Although you do not know who was in the pod, you assume it is an enemy of the Empire who escaped. Any enemy of the Empire could be an ally to you.

You look in the direction where you last sighted the falling escape pod, and see a thin wisp of smoke rising up beyond a nearby hill. Believing the pod might be on fire, you run as fast as you can over the hill.

Smoke billows out of the open door of the crashed escape pod. You try to see inside, but the smoke is too thick.

"Is anybody in there?" you shout as you rush up to the door. No answer comes from within the pod. Suddenly, the smoke overwhelms you. Doubling over, and trying to catch your breath, you notice a wide trail leading from the pod door. It looks like someone has dragged a large, heavy body from the pod.

The trail leads behind the wide trunk of a massive tree. Following the trail, you wipe the soot from your face. Momentarily distracted, you nearly walk into a Hutt.

The Hutt holds an Imperial blaster rifle in one of his three-fingered hands. The rifle is aimed at your head.

Choose to hypnotize, persuade, or disarm the Hutt. If you choose to persuade, choose with or without Power.

To hypnotize the Hutt (using Power)*: Choose your Hypnotism Power. Add your Jedi# + your stealth# +1 to your

Power's low-resist# for your confront#. Roll the 6-dice to hypnotize the Hutt into lowering his weapon.

> *If your confront# is equal to or more than your roll#,* add the difference +3 to your MP total. The Hutt lowers his weapon, giving you a chance to ask him a few questions. You may now proceed.
>
> *If your confront# is less than your roll#,* subtract the difference from your MP total. The Hutt's finger tenses on the blaster trigger. This is not a good sign. You must now disarm him (below).

Note: This counts as one of three Power uses you are allowed on this Mission.

To persuade the Hutt (using Power)*: Choose your Persuasion Power. Your charm# + your Power's mid-resist# + your Jedi# is your confront#. Roll the 6-dice to quickly convince the Hutt that you are only trying to help.

> *If your confront# is equal to or more than your roll#,* add the difference +4 to your MP total. The Hutt is willing to listen and lowers his rifle. You may now proceed.
>
> *If your confront# is less than your roll#,* subtract the difference from your MP total. The Hutt still thinks you are out to get him. You will now have to disarm him before he gets *you* (below).

Note: This counts as one of three Power uses you are allowed on this Mission.

To persuade the Hutt (without Power): Your charm# +2 is your confront#. Roll the 6-dice to tell the Hutt you were only trying to help any escape-pod survivors.

If your confront# is equal to or more than your roll#, add the difference +4 to your MP total. The Hutt is willing to listen and lowers the rifle. You may now proceed.

If your confront# is less than your roll#, subtract the difference from your MP total. The Hutt believes you were hoping to *kill* any survivors, and prepares to fire his blaster rifle. You must now disarm the Hutt (below).

To disarm the Hutt: Add your stealth# to your strength# +6 for your confront#. Roll the 12-dice to kick the blaster rifle out of the massive Hutt's hand.

If your confront# is equal to or more than your roll#, add the difference +4 to your MP total. Your foot connects with the back of the Hutt's hand, knocking the blaster rifle out of his reach. You may now proceed.

If your confront# is less than your roll#, subtract the difference from your MP total. Your kick missed the Hutt and he was able to fire a blast, nearly neutralizing you. Subtract 1 from your confront# for your new confront#. Roll the 6-dice to grab hold of the Hutt's rifle and tear it from his grip.

If your new confront# is equal to or more than your roll#, add the difference to your MP total. Yanking the blaster rifle from the Hutt, you toss the weapon to the ground. You may now proceed.

If your new confront# is less than your roll#, subtract the difference from your MP total. Repeat this confront with your new confront# until you have disarmed the Hutt. When he no longer holds the rifle, you may proceed.

Facing the Hutt, you raise your empty hands away from your weapon belt. "I don't want to fight you!" you proclaim. "I just want to know if you are the one who escaped from the Lambda shuttle!"

"Who wants to know?" the Hutt asks, narrowing his large eyes at you.

"I'm with the Rebel Alliance," you reveal. "If you're in trouble with the Imperials, maybe I can help you!"

"You're with the Rebellion?" the Hutt asks in disbelief. "Wait a minute! Were you flying one of the ships that attacked the Lambda?"

"Yes, but only after the Lambda fired upon us," you answer. "My comrades' ships were disabled and my ship was damaged in the battle. I had to make an emergency landing not far from here. The other Rebels will come looking for us as soon as their ships are recharged."

"Then I offer you my thanks." The Hutt smiles. "My name is Boonda. If you hadn't attacked the Lambda, those Imperials would have carved me up for breakfast!"

"I'm here to find out if something has happened to the Vactooine mining colony, Boonda," you explain. "More

Rebels are on their way. Do you know if the Empire has taken over this planet?"

Before Boonda can answer, a stormtrooper steps out from behind a nearby tree. "Stop where you are!" the trooper shouts.

A second stormtrooper appears from the other side of the wide tree. The two stormtroopers may be scouts for more Imperial forces. You must stop the stormtroopers from alerting any other Imperial soldiers of your presence on Vactooine. You must also stop them from killing you.

Choose to combat both stormtroopers with or without Power. If you choose to combat without Power, choose to combat both stormtroopers at once, or one at a time.

To combat both stormtroopers (using Power)*: Choose your Object Movement Power or your Sleep Power. Your Power's low-resist# + your Jedi# +1 is your confront#. Roll the 6-dice to either cause a heavy branch to fall on the troopers' heads or make them fall asleep.

> *If your confront# is equal to or more than your roll#,* add the difference +5 to your MP total. The stormtroopers are knocked out before they hit the ground. Boonda is amazed by your talent. You may now proceed.
>
> *If your confront# is less than your roll#,* subtract the difference from your MP total. You have failed with Power. "If you hadn't taken away my blaster rifle, *I* would have just *shot* those guys!" Boonda mutters, clearly not impressed. You must combat the stormtroopers without Power, either both at once or one at a time (below).

Note: This counts as one of three Power uses you are allowed on this Mission.

To combat both stormtroopers at once (without Power): Choose your weapon. Add your weaponry# to your weapon's far-range# for your confront#. Roll the 6-dice to shoot a heavy branch hanging above both troopers.

If your confront# is equal to or more than your roll#, add the difference +4 to your MP total. The branch crashes to the ground, knocking out both stormtroopers. You may now proceed.

If your confront# is less than your roll#, subtract the difference from your MP total. You have missed the branch and must proceed to combat one stormtrooper at a time (below).

To combat one stormtrooper at a time (without Power): Choose your weapon. Add your weaponry# to your weapon's mid-range# for your confront#. Roll the 6-dice to shoot the first stormtrooper.

If your confront# is equal to or more than your roll#, add the difference +3 to your MP total. The first stormtrooper is neutralized. Repeat this confront to combat the second stormtrooper. When both troopers are neutralized, you may proceed.

If your confront# is less than your roll#, subtract the difference from your MP total. Now add +6 to your confront# for your new confront#. Roll the 12-dice to shoot the stormtrooper.

If your new confront# is equal to or more than your roll#, add the difference to your MP total. If necessary, repeat this confront with your new confront# to combat the second stormtrooper. When both troopers are neutralized, you may proceed.

If your new confront# is less than your roll#, subtract the difference from your MP total. Repeat this confront with your new confront# until you have neutralized both stormtroopers. When both white-armored soldiers lie silent beneath the tree, you may proceed.

Slithering to the fallen stormtroopers, Boonda picks up a blaster rifle. "There isn't any Imperial base on Vactooine," the Hutt informs you. "These stormtroopers must have come from the Lambda shuttle. The shuttle might have landed or crashed near here."

Motioning Boonda to follow, you move cautiously from one tree trunk to the next, searching for signs of other stormtroopers. "If there isn't an Imperial base on this planet, what brought the Lambda to the Vactooine system?" you inquire.

"The Imperials hope to find their Star Destroyer *Decimator,*" Boonda answers. "Until recently, I owned a droid factory. Something went wrong with my droids. They killed my partner, Olag Greck. Then they took over the *Decimator* and its Imperial droids."

"Renegade droids?" you remark, startled by the Hutt's information. "Maybe that explains why the shipment of metal never arrived on Yavin Four. Do you think it's possible your droids might have attacked Vactooine's mining colony?"

Boonda nods his massive head. "If they could take over a Star Destroyer, they're capable of anything!"

Catching sight of a tall, white object amidst the trees, you realize you've sighted the crashed Lambda. "There's the shuttle!" you whisper excitedly to Boonda. Buried deep in the ground, a shattered transparisteel window appears to be the only thing left from the cockpit. Although the triangular upper stabilizer and starboard wing are still in one piece, the portside wing is nothing but mangled plastoid fragments. "It looks like the Imperials had a rough landing."

Narrowing his eyes on the felled trees and ruined shuttle, Boonda whispers, "If we hadn't run into those two stormtroopers, I wouldn't believe *anyone* could survive a crash like this."

"How many troops were on the shuttle?" you ask.

"Eighteen troopers and two officers," Boonda recalls.

"I'd better see if anyone else survived," you declare, reaching for your weapon and moving toward the crashed Lambda.

The bodies of a number of stormtroopers have been laid out on the ground, apparently dragged from the wreckage of the Lambda. They will not be a threat. But others may have survived. You move to the other side of the crashed ship to see if they're still alive.

Sure enough, two Imperial officers and a stormtrooper are standing in the shuttle's crash path, preparing to launch an emergency distress beacon. Before you can react, they launch the beacon.

You must destroy the emergency distress beacon before it carries a message to the Empire.

To destroy the distress beacon: Choose your weapon. Add your weapon's far-range# to your weaponry# for your confront#. Roll the 6-dice to fire at the rising beacon.

> *If your confront# is equal to or more than your roll#,* add the difference to your MP total. The missile carrying the beacon explodes high above the Vactooine forest. You may now proceed.
>
> *If your confront# is less than your roll#,* subtract the difference from your MP total. Repeat the confront until you have destroyed the launched beacon. Then you may proceed.

The stormtrooper and two Imperial officers catch sight of you near the shuttle. The Imperial officers are unarmed, having left their weapons aside as they assembled the beacon launcher. The stormtrooper raises his blaster rifle to fire at you.

You must combat the armed stormtrooper.

To combat the armed stormtrooper: Choose your weapon. Your weapon's mid-range# +1 is your confront#. Roll the 6-dice to fire upon the trooper.

> *If your confront# is equal to or more than your roll#,* add the difference to your MP total. The neutralized stormtrooper falls to the ground. The Imperial officers have not yet begun to flee. You may now proceed.

If your confront# is less than your roll#, subtract the difference from your MP total. Add +1 to your confront# for your new confront#.

If your new confront# is equal to or more than your roll#, the stormtrooper has been defeated. But the Imperial officers have begun to flee. This will affect your next confront.

If your new confront# is less than your roll#, subtract the difference from your MP total and repeat this confront until you have neutralized the stormtroopers. The Imperial officers have begun to flee. This will affect your next confront.

If you can capture the two Imperial officers, they may provide you with information about the Empire's interest on Vactooine. If you cannot capture the two officers, you must combat them.

Choose to capture or combat the two Imperial officers. If you choose to combat, choose to combat them both at once or one at a time. If you choose to capture, choose to do so with or without Power.

To capture the two Imperial officers (using Power)*: Choose your Capture Power. If the Imperial officers have begun to flee, your charm# + your Power's mid-resist# + your Jedi# is your confront#. If the Imperial officers have not begun to flee, your charm# + your Power's low-resist# + your Jedi# is your confront#. Roll the 6-dice to lure the officers into surrendering immediately.

If your confront# is equal to or more than your roll#, add the difference +4 to your MP total. The Imperial officers surrender but they still refuse to talk. You may now proceed.

If your confront# is less than your roll#, subtract the difference from your MP total. The officers ignore your command and reach for their blaster rifles. You must combat them both at once (below).

Note: This counts as one of three Power uses you are allowed on this Mission.

To capture the two Imperial officers (without Power): If the Imperial officers have begun to flee, your stealth# +1 is your confront#. If they have not yet begun to flee, your charm# +3 is your confront#. Roll the 6-dice to convince the officers to surrender immediately.

If your confront# is equal to or more than your roll#, add the difference +4 to your MP total. The two officers surrender but they still refuse to talk. You may now proceed.

If your confront# is less than your roll#, subtract the difference from your MP total. The officers ignore your command and reach for their blaster rifles. You must combat both Imperial officers at once (below).

To combat both Imperial officers at once: Your skill# + your strength# +1 is your confront#. If the Imperial officers have not yet begun to flee, roll the 6-dice to throw a grenade at the officers. If the Imperial officers have begun to flee, roll the 12-dice.

If your confront# is equal to or more than your roll#, add the difference +3 to your MP total. The grenade explodes knocking the two officers to the ground. You may now proceed.

If your confront# is less than your roll#, subtract the difference from your MP total. Both officers leap away from the explosion and grab hold of their blaster rifles. You must combat one Imperial officer at a time (below).

To combat one Imperial officer at a time: Choose your weapon. If the Imperial officers have begun to flee, your weaponry# + your weapon's far-range# is your confront#. If they have not yet begun to flee, add your weaponry# to your weapon's mid-range# for your confront#. Roll the 6-dice to stun the first officer.

If your confront# is equal to or more than your roll#, add the difference +2 to your MP total. The first officer is knocked off his feet. Repeat this confront to attack the second officer. When both officers are defeated, you may proceed.

If your confront# is less than your roll#, subtract the difference from your MP total. You missed and must fire again. Repeat this confront until you have defeated both officers. Then you may proceed.

The two Imperial officers won't be talking to you for awhile. Still, you have defeated the surviving Imperials on Vactooine.

Add 30 MP to your MP total (50 MP for Advanced Level players).

After you tie the two Imperial officers to a tree, Boonda the Hutt approaches from the wrecked shuttle. "They're not going anywhere," Boonda announces. "We can come back for them later."

A quick check on your data pad confirms the mining colony is located several kilometers west of your present position. Looking up, you state, "I need to get to the mining colony, Boonda." Much to your surprise, the Hutt seems to have vanished.

"Over here!" Boonda calls from some nearby trees. You find Boonda standing beside a large land vehicle. "I remember this vehicle from the Lambda's cargo bay! It must have been thrown clear of the crash. It has some dents, but it seems to be in good shape."

Climbing in, you declare, "I'm going to the mining colony. Do you want to help me, Boonda?"

"Try stopping me!" the Hutt answers, hoisting his bulky body onto the back of the vehicle.

To speed to the mining colony: Choose your vehicle (it must be capable of land travel). Add your vehicle's speed# to your vehicle's distance# for your confront#. Roll the 6-dice to speed out of the forest . . . and into the Vactooine mining colony.

> *If your confront# is equal to or more than your roll#,* add the difference +5 to your MP total. Within minutes, you reach the outskirts of the mining colony. You may now proceed.

If your confront# is less than your roll#, subtract the difference from your MP total. Boonda's weight is too much of a strain on your vehicle's repulsorlift engines, causing the vehicle to stall. Subtract your vehicle's weaponry# and add your skill# to your confront# for your new confront#. Roll the 6-dice to channel energy from your vehicle's weaponry to your vehicle's engines.

> *If your new confront# is equal to or more than your roll#,* add the difference to your MP total. The adjustment to your repulsorlift engines is a success and you soon reach the mining colony.
>
> *If your new confront# is less than your roll#,* subtract the difference from your MP total. Repeat this confront with your new confront# until you have sighted the mining colony. Then you may proceed.

Parking the land vehicle at the edge of a high cliff, you gaze down at the mining colony below. The colony is made up of a dozen modular buildings, including the colonists' apartments, two long warehouses, a refinery, and a small spaceport.

On a broad plateau north of the spaceport, small figures can be seen moving around an immense starship. The ship is a Victory Star Destroyer.

"That's the *Decimator*!" Boonda exclaims.

Raising your macrobinoculars to your eyes, you scan the Star Destroyer. "I think we've located your droids, too," you observe. "There must be hundreds of them. It looks like they're transferring equipment from the *Decimator* to one of the colony's warehouses."

"Any sign of the miners?" Boonda asks.

"I can only see droids from here. If we're going to find out what happened to the miners, we should search those buildings."

Suddenly, blaster fire erupts from behind you, causing you to duck. One of the shots hits Boonda's left arm, causing the Hutt to shout in pain. Before risking a glance at your unseen attacker, you must leap out of firing range.

To leap out of firing range: Your strength# + your stealth# is your confront#. Roll the 6-dice to leap for cover.

> *If your confront# is equal to or more than your roll#,* add the difference to your MP total. You dive behind a large rock and may now proceed.
>
> *If your confront# is less than your roll#,* subtract the difference from your MP total. You stumbled over Boonda's tail. Repeat this confront until you have reached protective cover behind a rock. Then you may proceed.

"Are you hurt, Boonda?" you shout from behind the rock. A tree stands beside it.

"I'll be okay," the thick-skinned Hutt answers, "but my arm will hurt for awhile. Can you see who's shooting at us?"

Peering over the top of the rock, you see an Imperial probe droid hanging in the air over the fallen Hutt. You should have known the droids would set up sentries around the mining colony. Adjusting its targeting sensor, the probe droid aims its laser cannon at you.

You must prevent the Imperial probe droid from transmitting a message to the other droids. If you're very careful, you might be able to destroy the droid without using any weapons.

Combating the droid with a weapon might be easier, but it also might draw the attention of other droids. The probe droid can be destroyed with one shot to its computer head, but it's a difficult shot. Another option is to first shoot the droid's broadcast antennae, then its rotation joint.

Choose to evade or combat the prode droid. If you choose to combat, choose to shoot the probe droid's computer head or target the droid's broadcast antennae. You may use Power with any of these options. Choose now.

To evade the probe droid (using Power)*: Choose your Evasion Power. Your stealth# + your Power's low-resist# + your Jedi# + your strength# is your confront#. Roll the 6-dice to leap into the tree and climb to the highest branches.

> *If your confront# is equal to or more than your roll#,* add the difference +9 to your MP total. The probe droid tries to follow you up into the tree, but the branches are too thick. The droid damages its antennae and laser cannon, then tangles its manipulator appendages in the tree branches. The probe droid is unable to move. You may now proceed.

If your confront# is less than your roll#, subtract the difference from your MP total. The probe droid does not follow you up into the tree, but moves through the air to get a better shot at you. You must proceed to shoot the Imperial probe droid's computer head, with or without Power (below).

Note: This counts as one of three Power uses you are allowed on this Mission.

To evade the probe droid (without Power): Add your stealth# to your strength# for your confront#. Roll the 6-dice to leap up into the tree, scrambling up the branches.

If your confront# is equal to or more than your roll#, add the difference +8 to your MP total. The probe droid tries to follow you up into the tree, but the branches are too thick. The droid damages its antennae and laser cannon, then tangles its manipulator appendages in the tree branches. The probe droid is unable to move. You may now proceed.

If your confront# is less than your roll#, subtract the difference from your MP total. The probe droid does not follow you up into the tree, but moves through the air to get a better shot at you. You must proceed to shoot the Imperial probe droid's computer head, with or without Power (below).

To shoot the Imperial droid's computer head (using Power)*: Choose your weapon and your Aim Power. Your weaponry# + your weapon's mid-range# + your Power's low-resist# + your Jedi# +3 is your confront#. Roll the 12-dice.

If your confront# is equal to or more than your roll#, add the difference +10 to your MP total. The droid's manipulator appendages twitch as its head erupts into a fireball. The probe droid falls in a heap on the ground. You may proceed.

If your confront# is less than your roll#, subtract the difference from your MP total. The droid shifts in the air, avoiding your shot and drifting closer to your position. The droid fires at the rock in front of you and you must proceed to shoot its broadcast antennae, with or without Power (below).

Note: This counts as one of three Power uses you are allowed on this Mission.

To shoot the Imperial probe droid's computer head (without Power): Choose your weapon. Add your weaponry# to your weapon's mid-range# +3 for your confront#. Roll the 12-dice to shoot the droid's armored head.

If your confront# is equal to or more than your roll#, add the difference +10 to your MP total. The droid's manipulator appendages twitch as its head erupts into a fireball. The probe droid falls in a heap on the ground. You may proceed.

If your confront# is less than your roll#, subtract the difference from your MP total. The droid shifts in the air, avoiding your shot and drifting closer to your position. The droid fires at the rock in front of you and you must proceed to shoot its broadcast antennae, with or without Power (below).

To shoot the Imperial droid's broadcast antennae (using Power)*: Choose your weapon and your Aim Power. Your weaponry# + your weapon's close-range# + your Power's low-resist# + your Jedi# +2 is your confront#. Roll the 6-dice to shoot the two antennae extending above the droid's head.

If your confront# is equal to or more than your roll#, add the difference +5 to your MP total. The antennae are destroyed. Repeat this confront to take another shot at the droid's rotation joint. After the joint explodes, separating the droid's head from its lower body, you may proceed.

If your confront# is less than your roll#, subtract 5 MP from your MP total. You've missed. Repeat this confront until you have shot the probe droid's broadcast antennae and rotation joint.

***Note:** This counts as one of three Power uses you are allowed on this Mission.

To target the Imperial probe droid's broadcast antennae (without Power): Choose your weapon. Add your weaponry# to your weapon's close-range# for your confront#. Roll the 6-dice to shoot the two antennae extending above the droid's head.

If your confront# is equal to or more than your roll#, add the difference +4 to your MP total. The antennae are destroyed. Repeat this confront to take another shot at the droid's rotation joint. After the joint explodes, separating the droid's head from its lower body, you may proceed.

If your confront# is less than your roll#, subtract the difference from your MP total. You have missed the shot. Add +1 to your confront# for your new confront#. Roll the 6-dice again to shoot the probe droid.

> *If your new confront# is equal to or more than your roll#,* add the difference to your MP total. If necessary, repeat this confront to take another shot at the droid's rotation joint. After the droid's body is cleaved in half, you may proceed.
>
> *If your new confront# is less than your roll#,* subtract the difference from your MP total. Repeat this confront with your new confront# until you have shot the probe droid's broadcast antennae and rotation joint. Once you have defeated the probe droid, you may proceed.

As you run to check on Boonda the Hutt, you hear the roar of engines firing from the mining colony. A quick glance through your macrobinoculars allows you to see a number of small repulsorlift vehicles moving toward you.

"The other droids seem to have been alerted to our position, Boonda!" you inform the Hutt.

"Perhaps the probe droid transmitted a message after all, or maybe the droids caught sight of your battle with the probe droid," Boonda muses. "Either way, we've been found out! I'm afraid I'll only slow you down. I could try distracting the droids from you while you try finding the colonists!"

"In that case, you take our vehicle and I'll go on foot," you urge. "If you drive away from here, the droids might follow you while I descend this cliff. I'll try meeting you at the colony's spaceport in thirty minutes."

"Let's hope your Rebel friends arrive here soon," Boonda says as he slithers to the vehicle. "And remember to keep an eye out for more Imperials!" Clambering onto the vehicle, the Hutt throws his tail onto the passenger seat. Hitting the ignition, Boonda blasts away, sending up a high trail of dust.

Looking down from the clifftop, you see the droids' vehicles veer away, trying to follow Boonda's dust trail. You must now descend the cliff to reach the mining colony.

Choose to climb down the cliff or slide down a steep dirt path.

To climb down the cliff: Your strength# +1 is your confront#. Roll the 6-dice to make your way down the cliff.

> *If your confront# is equal to or more than your roll#,* add the difference +2 to your MP total. It was an easy climb to the bottom and you may now proceed.
>
> *If your confront# is less than your roll#,* subtract the difference from your MP total. A loose rock slips from under your foot, sending you tumbling from your foothold. You must proceed to slide down the steep dirt path (below).

To slide down a steep dirt path: Your stealth# +1 is your confront#. Roll the 6-dice to lean back and slide down to the bottom of the dirt path.

> *If your confront# is equal to or more than your roll#,* add the difference to your MP total. You are breathless and covered in dirt when you reach the ground, but you have survived in one piece. You may now proceed.
>
> *If your confront# is less than your roll#,* subtract the difference from your MP total. Repeat the confront until you have reached the bottom of the dirt path, then you may proceed.

Running from the bottom of the cliff, you stick to the shadows, trying to keep out of sight from any patrolling droids. As you approach one of the colony outbuildings, the ground collapses beneath your feet. You fall into a deep hole.

Crashing down through the hole, you hit a rocky surface. You are surrounded by darkness. You realize the droids must have prepared traps around the colony, digging deep holes to capture any trespassers. Lighting a small glow rod, you see you have fallen into a mining cave.

Unable to climb out the way you fell in, you move forward through the cave, trying to find a way out. The walls of the cave are composed of dark gray stone. As you approach a turning point in the cave, you hear a mechanical whirring sound from around a corner.

Thinking there might be a droid waiting for you, you turn off your glow rod and draw your weapon. Slowly moving around the corner, you see two red electronic photoreceptors glowing in the darkness. The distance between the glowing eyes indicates there are two droids in front of you.

You must evade or combat the two droids. Choose to evade them using Power or combat them without using Power. If you choose combat, choose to combat both droids at once or one at a time.

To evade the security droids (using Power)*: Choose your Camouflage Power or Evasion Power. Your Power's low-resist# + your Jedi# + your stealth# +3 is your confront#. Roll the 12-dice to virtually blend into the cavern walls.

> *If your confront# is equal to or more than your roll#,* add the difference +3 to your MP total. Unable to see you, the two droids do not detect your passage through the cave. You may now proceed.

> *If your confront# is less than your roll#,* subtract the difference from your MP total. The droids are equipped with sophisticated infrared photoreceptors and are able to see you in the dark. Hearing the droids' motors whir as they reach for their weapons, you realize you must combat both droids at once (below).

Note: This counts as one of three Power uses you are allowed on this Mission.

To combat both droids at once (without Power): Add your stealth# to your strength# for your confront#. Putting on your infrared goggles, you see two K4 security droids standing in front of you. Roll the 6-dice to leap between the two droids and grab their firing arms.

If your confront# is equal to or more than your roll#, add the difference +5 to your MP total. You force the droids to aim their blasters at each others' heads, and the startled droids accidentally destroy one another. You may now proceed.

If your confront# is less than your roll#, subtract the difference from your MP total. Both droids twist their arms free of your grip, bringing up their blasters to fire at you. You must combat one K4 security droid at a time (below).

To combat one K4 security droid at a time (without Power): Choose your weapon. Add your weaponry# to your weapon's close-range# for your confront#. Roll the 6-dice to shoot the first K4 security droid.

If your confront# is equal to or more than your roll#, add the difference +2 to your MP total. The first droid is blown to bits. Repeat this confront to combat the second security droid. When both K4 units are defeated, you may proceed.

If your confront# is less than your roll#, subtract the difference from your MP total. You missed the droid, hitting the cavern wall instead. Add +5 to your confront# for your new confront#. Roll the 12-dice to shoot the K4 unit.

If your new confront# is equal to or more than your roll#, add the difference to your MP total. If necessary, repeat this confront with your new confront# to combat the second droid. When both K4 units are nothing but scorched circuitry, you may proceed.

If your new confront# is less than your roll#, subtract the difference from your MP total. Repeat this confront with your new confront# until you have destroyed both droids. When both K4s have been reduced to scrap metal, you may proceed.

At the end of the cavern corridor, you reach a ladder that extends upwards into a mineshaft. Climbing to the top of the ladder, you step onto a platform and walk to a locked hatchway.

The hatchway may be your best route of escape. Choose to hot-wire the lock, kick the hatch open, or blast the lock off.

To hot-wire the lock: Your skill# +2 is your confront#. Roll the 6-dice to neatly pop the lock off the vent.

If your confront# is equal to or more than your roll#, add the difference to your MP total. The hatch flies open. You may now proceed.

If your confront# is less than your roll#, subtract the difference from your MP total. Your wiring doesn't work. You must proceed to kick the hatch open (below).

To kick the hatch open: Your strength# +1 is your confront#. Roll the 6-dice to kick a hole in the vent.

If your confront# is equal to or more than your roll#, add the difference to your MP total. With a single kick, your foot knocks the hatch off its hinges. You may now proceed.

If your confront# is less than your roll#, subtract the difference from your MP total. Stubbing your toe, you decide to try kicking with your other foot. Add +1 to your confront# for your new confront#. Roll the 6-dice to launch another kick at the vent.

If your new confront# is equal to or more than your roll#, add the difference to your MP total. The hatch is open. You may proceed.

If your new confront# is less than your roll#, subtract the difference from your MP total. You have stubbed your toes on both feet and should consider getting a new pair of boots. Proceed to blast the lock off (below).

To blast the lock off: Choose your weapon. Add your weaponry# to your weapon's close-range# for your confront#. Roll the 6-dice to shoot the lock clean off the hatch.

If your confront# is equal to or more than your roll#, add the difference to your MP total. The blast takes out both the lock and most of the hatch. You may now proceed.

If your confront# is less than your roll#, subtract the difference from your MP total. Repeat this confront until you have blown away the lock. Then you may proceed.

Passing through the hatchway, you find yourself in a corridor with plastoid walls. It appears you are in the basement of one of the colony buildings.

Finding an open door, you peer into a room illuminated by a pale blue light. The room has no windows, but a large air vent is set into the wall below the ceiling, bringing air to the basement chamber. Stepping quietly into the room, you find a reptilian alien with long, pointed ears. He is sitting with his back to you, working at a computer console.

Believing the alien must be a captive of the droids, you say, "Excuse me?"

"AAAGH!" yells the startled alien. Spinning to face you, he reveals himself to have a small mouth filled with sharp teeth. "Who are you? Where did you come from?"

"I'm with the Rebellion!" you reply. "I'm here to rescue you from the droids."

"A Rebel? Here to rescue me?" the alien replies, his eyes wide with disbelief. The alien backs up toward the computer.

Suddenly, a pig-faced Gamorrean guard enters through the door behind you. The Gamorrean carries a lethal vibro-ax. As the porcine guard moves toward you, you realize he intends to kill you.

It is possible the Gamorrean is a prisoner of the droids, but believes you are an invader. You do not have time to explain yourself. Choose to combat the Gamorrean with or without using Power. Try to only stun the creature.

To combat the Gamorrean (using Power)*: Choose your Object Movement Power or Hypnotism Power. Your Power's mid-resist# + your Jedi# +1 is your confront#. Roll the 6-dice to either force the Gamorrean to strike himself in the head with the handle of his vibro-ax or make him think he's a rock.

> *If your confront# is equal to or more than your roll#,* add the difference +5 to your MP total. If your chose Object Movement, the Gamorrean hits himself and falls unconscious to the floor; if you chose Hypnotism, he falls to the floor thinking he's a rock. You may now proceed.
>
> *If your confront# is less than your roll#,* subtract the difference from your MP total. Gamorreans have notoriously thick skulls and your Power did not work. You must combat the guard without using Power (below).

****Note:*** This counts as one of three Power uses you are allowed on this Mission.

To combat the Gamorrean (without Power): Choose your weapon. Add your weaponry# to your weapon's close-range# for your confront#. Roll the 6-dice to stun the advancing Gamorrean.

> *If your confront# is equal to or more than your roll#,* add the difference +4 to your MP total. The guard topples to the floor and you may proceed.
>
> *If your confront# is less than your roll#,* subtract the difference from your MP total. Repeat the confront until

you have defeated the Gamorrean. Then you may proceed.

For defeating the guard, reward yourself with 15 MP (35 MP for Advanced Level players).

Bending down to check on the Gamorrean, you find him breathing steadily. "He'll be okay," you inform the pointy-eared alien. "I don't understand why he attacked me. It sounds ridiculous, but do you think he works for the droids?"

"Actually, I know a lot about this Gamorrean," the alien replies. "His name is Xob. He works for me."

Turning to face the alien, you find yourself staring down the length of his raised blaster pistol. "But . . . I thought you were one of the miners, in danger of the droids!" you stammer, raising your hands.

The alien laughs. "My name is Olag Greck. As of today, I *own* this mining operation! You happened to stumble into my new office." Greck pushes a button on the computer console's comm unit. "Greck to Forwun! I have an intruder in my office. Come here at once!"

"Olag Greck?" you repeat. The name sounds familiar. Suddenly, you remember Boonda the Hutt mentioning his former partner. "But I heard that Olag Greck was killed by the renegade droids!"

Greck chuckles. "I'm glad to know my vanishing act worked! Once I gained control of Boonda's droids, it was easy to fake my own death to prevent anyone from suspecting me. Too bad you've stumbled onto my plan to take over the Vactooine mining operation, Rebel! But we'll put you to good use with the miners."

"*You* took over Boonda's droids?" you inquire, trying to buy time and gain information. "I find *that* hard to believe!"

"It's true!" Greck insists. "I altered a 1-2 unit's programming to do my bidding. Then I modified his broadband antennae to transmit a powerful signal to every other droid within his broadcast range. The signal made the droids obey my every command!"

Hearing the clanking approach of metal feet from the hallway, you realize you must evade Olag Greck before the droids arrive.

To evade Olag Greck: Add your stealth# to your strength# +3 for your confront#. Roll the 12-dice to leap up to the air vent.

> *If your confront# is equal to or more than your roll#,* add the difference to your MP total. In a single bound, you leap into the air vent, racing out of the warehouse the same way you came in. You may now proceed.
>
> *If your confront# is less than your roll#,* subtract the difference from your MP total. Olag Greck manages to fire his blaster, narrowly missing you. Repeat the confront until you have escaped into the air vent. Then you may proceed.

Scrambling through the dark vent, you hear Olag cursing in the room behind you, shouting new orders into his comm unit. Checking your chronometer, you realize nearly half an hour has passed since you last saw Boonda. With any luck, the Hutt should be arriving at the colony spaceport in just a few minutes.

Reaching the end of the vent, you tumble out onto the ground. Looking behind you, it appears you have emerged from the mining colony's spaceport supply building.

"There's the intruder!" reports a cold, mechanical voice. Turning to look down the length of the warehouse exterior, you see a black-metal 1-2 unit standing with a tall ASP-19. The 1-2 unit points in your direction and commands, "Get him!"

As you prepare to run away, you see two other ASP-19s approaching your position. The three ASPs have you surrounded.

Each of the ASP-19s appears to be carrying a glow rod. Suddenly, their rods ignite and extend, and you realize the droids are not carrying mere portable lamps. The ASP-19s are all wielding lightsabers.

The three droids lurch forward, backing you up against the building wall, blocking your path of escape. Their lightsabers make a deadly humming sound as the droids press closer toward you.

Choose to evade or combat the ASP-19s. If you choose evasion, choose to evade with or without using Power. If you choose combat, choose to combat all three ASP-19s at once or one at a time.

To evade the ASP-19s (using Power)*: Choose your Evasion Power, Confusion Power, or Deception Power. Your stealth# + your Power's low-resist# is your confront#. Roll the 6-dice to slip past the droids and run through the spaceport.

If your confront# is equal to or more than your roll#, add the difference +5 to your MP total. The ASP-19s accidentally carve out the warehouse wall as you deftly avoid their attack. You may now proceed.

If your confront# is less than your roll#, subtract the difference from your MP total. You can't get by the droids. You must proceed to evade the ASP-19s without Power or combat them (below).

***Note:** This counts as one of three Power uses you are allowed on this Mission.

To evade the ASP-19s (without Power): Add your stealth# to your strength# +3 for your confront#. Roll the 12-dice to leap over the menacing droids.

If your confront# is equal to or more than your roll#, add the difference +7 to your MP total. The droids are still searching for you as you run through the spaceport. You may now proceed.

If your confront# is less than your roll#, subtract the difference from your MP total. Leaping into the air, your leg catches on an ASP's visor, causing you to tumble. Rising from the ground, you must combat all three ASP-19s at once (below).

To combat all three ASP-19s at once: Choose your weapon. Add your weaponry# to your weapon's mid-range# +4 for your confront#. Roll the 12-dice to fire a shot at one ASP-19's left leg.

If your confront# is equal to or more than your roll#, add the difference +9 to your MP total. The ASP-19's leg explodes from underneath him, causing him to topple toward the other two ASP-19s. As the damaged droid falls, he accidentally drags his lightsaber through the other two droids. The three ASP-19s are destroyed. You may now proceed.

If your confront# is less than your roll#, subtract the difference from your MP total. Missing the droid's leg, you must proceed to combat the ASP-19s one at a time (below).

To combat the ASP-19s one at a time: Choose your weapon. Add your weaponry# to your weapon's close-range# for your confront#. Roll the 6-dice to blast the nearest ASP-19's head off.

If your confront# is equal to or more than your roll#, add the difference +3 to your MP total. The droid's head ruptures in a shower of sparks and you may now proceed. Repeat this confront to combat the next droid. When you have defeated all three ASP-19s, you may proceed.

If your confront# is less than your roll#, subtract the difference from your MP total. The blast bounces off the droid's heavy armor plating. Add +1 to your confront# for your new confront#. Roll the 6-dice again to fire another blast at the ASP-19.

If your new confront# is equal to or more than your roll#, add the difference to your MP total. The ASP-19 buckles over, toppling to the ground. If necessary, repeat this confront to combat the second and third ASP-19. After all three droids are destroyed, you may proceed.

If your new confront# is less than your roll#, subtract the difference from your MP total. Repeat this confront with your new confront# until you have defeated all three ASP-19s. Then you may proceed.

Having defeated three lightsaber-wielding ASP-19s, add 30 MP to your MP total (60 MP for Advanced Level players).

Suddenly, a land vehicle races to the colony spaceport, heading straight for you. The 1-2 unit leaps out of the way as the landspeeder roars up beside you. You recognize the driver immediately.

"Boonda!" you shout as the vehicle screeches to a stop near you.

"Get in!" Boonda calls out as he brings up a blaster rifle. Without warning, the engine stalls. "Oops!" says the befuddled Hutt.

The 1-2 unit cranes his neck forward, then shakes his head in genuine surprise. "Boonda the Hutt? Alive on Vactooine? But Master Greck told me you were dead!"

Seeing that the droid has lowered his blaster, Boonda shouts, "Something's wrong with your circuits, Wuntoo Forcee Forwun! You told me the droids killed Olag!"

"No!" the droid replies. "That can't be true!"

Realizing the 1-2 unit must be the droid Olag Greck mentioned, you shout, "Forwun — Olag has tricked you!

Use your broadband antennae to transmit a signal to the other droids. Tell them to drop their weapons."

You must convince Forwun you are telling the truth.

To convince Forwun you are telling the truth: Your charm# +5 is your confront#. Roll the 12-dice to explain how Olag Greck used Forwun to take over the other droids.

> *If your confront# is equal to or more than your roll#,* add the difference to your MP total. Realizing the truth, Forwun drops his blaster. You may now proceed.
>
> *If your confront# is less than your roll#,* subtract the difference from your MP total. Forwun doesn't believe you. He raises his weapon. Roll the 6-dice to try again.
>
> > *If you roll 1 or 2:* Forwun fires at you — and hits you in the arm. Subtract 20 MP from your MP total. Despite being injured, you continue to talk to Forwun as if nothing happened. He trusts you after this. You may proceed.
> >
> > *If you roll 3 or 4:* Forwun fires at you — and misses. You shoot back — and also miss. Subtract 10 MP from your MP total. In order to show him you are serious, you drop your weapon. He believes you after this. You may proceed.
> >
> > *If you roll 5 or 6:* Forwun fires at you — and misses. You shoot back — and hit his arm. His gun is knocked away from him, and you could easily finish him off. Instead, you again try to convince him

you are telling the truth. This time, he believes you. You may proceed.

Suddenly, dozens of armed droids come scrambling in your direction. Seeing their approach, Forwun raises one hand to his own head. Much to your surprise, all of the droids suddenly stop in their tracks and drop their weapons.

Olag Greck steps out from a nearby doorway. Beside him, Xob the Gamorrean lurches forward with his vibro-ax. A bandage is wrapped around the Gamorrean's thick head.

"Forwun!" Olag shouts at the black-metal droid. "What are you doing? You are *mine*. Finish them off!"

"It's over, Olag Greck," Forwun states. "I've used my broadband antennae to transmit a signal to the other droids. As we speak, they are releasing the miners from the warehouse. The droids and I will no longer obey your orders."

Olag Greck pushes Xob forward. "Kill Boonda and the Rebel!" Greck commands. "No one will foil my plan!"

As Xob approaches, Boonda asks, "You want me to just shoot him?"

"I can handle this guy," you proclaim.

You must combat Xob the Gamorrean.

To combat Xob: Choose your weapon. Add your weaponry# to your weapon's close-range# for your confront#. Roll the 6-dice to fire a devastating blast at the Gamorrean.

If your confront# is equal to or more than your roll#, add the difference to your MP total. The power of the blast lifts Olag's guard and sends him crashing against the ground. You may now proceed.

If your confront# is less than your roll#, subtract the difference from your MP total. You miss the Gamorrean and he nearly slices you in half. Subtract 1 from your confront# for your new confront#. Roll the 6-dice again to shoot Xob.

> *If your new confront# is equal to or more than your roll#,* add the difference to your MP total. Xob collapses with a heavy thud on the ground and you may proceed.
>
> *If your new confront# is less than your roll#,* subtract the difference from your MP total. Repeat this confront with your new confront# until you have defeated Xob. Then you may proceed.

You have rescued the mining colony and prevented the droids from causing any more havoc. Add 200 MP to your MP total (350 MP for Advanced Level players).

Following Boonda's command, the droids step forward and seize Olag Greck. "Stang! Let go of me!" Greck curses.

The sound of roaring engines above causes you to look overhead. Gazing upward, you see the fully powered X-wings descending from the sky.

"Look — my friends finally made it!" you exclaim to Boonda.

"Better late than never," the Hutt comments. Turning to

the black-metal 1-2 unit, Boonda says, "Forwun, you have a lot of explaining to do."

"If you give me a chance, sir, I believe I can explain," Forwun replies.

"Hold that thought until my friends land, Forwun," you suggest. "I'm sure they'll want to hear you, too."

The After-Mission

The sun was setting on the planet Vactooine. The Rebels and the miners stood in the shadow of the Star Destroyer *Decimator*. Facing the gathered crowd, the black-metal droid Wuntoo Forcee Forwun stood beside Boonda the Hutt on top of an elevated landing platform.

"My name is Boonda," the Hutt announced. "Until recently, I owned a droid factory. I also used to sell droids to the Empire. I assure you, my factory is gone and I will never work with the Empire again. I want to introduce you to Wuntoo Forcee Forwun. This droid claims he can explain everything that's happened over the past few days."

"Oh, great," muttered Han Solo from the crowd. "That's all we need is *another* talkative droid!" Chewbacca the Wookiee growled.

"Hush!" Princess Leia commanded.

Forwun stepped forward. "I wish to apologize to you all," he addressed the crowd. "My fellow droids and I never had any intention of causing any harm. We were the victims of Boonda the Hutt's partner, Olag Greck."

In the crowd, Artoo-Detoo rotated his domed head and beeped excitedly at See-Threepio.

"How *could* I forget Olag Greck, Artoo?" Threepio replied. "That villain nearly *demolished* us in the Karlarba system!"

"Shhh!" Princess Leia scolded, trying to listen to the traffic controller droid.

"After a long partnership with Boonda, Olag Greck wanted to run his own droid factory," Forwun continued. "He also wanted to do business with the Empire. When Greck learned the Star Destroyer *Decimator* was traveling to Boonda's Moon for a pickup, he concocted a sinister plan."

"I can't wait to hear *this*!" Boonda mumbled.

"Olag Greck secretly modified ASP droids for battle. Then he tampered with my circuitry, programming me to lead a revolt against Boonda," Forwun revealed. "He altered my broadband antennae to transmit a signal to other droids, scrambling their cogitative theory units so they would follow my lead."

"What a rascal, that Olag!" Boonda chuckled. "This plan is worthy of a Hutt!"

Forwun could not understand why Boonda found the story so amusing, but the droid continued his story. "Olag Greck had us try to kill Boonda and steal *Decimator* because he wanted to destroy Boonda's business with the Empire. Greck thought the Empire would put Boonda in prison for trying to sell defective droids. Greck believed he could start his own droid factory here on Vactooine, using the miners as slave laborers. He also intended on returning *Decimator* to the Empire, claiming he'd found it floating in space."

"Greck's plan was brilliant!" Boonda exclaimed. "The Empire would believe Olag had done them a great favor by locating their Star Destroyer. Then they would want to do business with him!"

"Although it was against my programming, I cannot deny I led the droids to Vactooine," Forwun concluded. "If you seek to punish anyone, take me, but I implore you not to damage my fellow droids. They are hard workers who never intended to cause any harm. Boonda the Hutt, our most gracious manufacturer, has granted us permission to remain on Vactooine and repair any damage we have caused."

"What about getting this ugly Star Destroyer off our planet?" one miner called out, causing some of the other colonists to laugh.

"The Star Destroyer *Decimator* is yours for scrap metal if you want it," Boonda stated. "But it might be put to better use by adding it to the Rebel fleet!"

In the crowd, Han Solo turned to Luke Skywalker and whispered, "Wouldn't that be something, kid? How would you like to fight the Empire with one of their own Star Destroyers!"

"Quiet, Solo!" Leia reprimanded.

The leader of the mining colony stepped forward to Boonda and Forwun. "We only want to help the Rebellion," the leader proclaimed. "Let them take this ship and use it to help crush the Imperial Navy!"

A loud cheer followed, rippling over the miners and Rebels like a great wave. Boonda the Hutt grinned and patted Forwun on the back. "Looks like they've accepted your apology, Forwun."

Following Boonda down from the landing platform, Forwun was happy to be greeted by BP-A1, BP-A2, and the repaired chef droid K-2PQ. The chef droid was missing two arms and his body had numerous dents. At the sight of the damaged droid, Boonda gasped.

"Hey, boss," K-2PQ rasped. "How would you like me to rustle up a snack for you?"

"K-2PQ!" the Hutt exclaimed. "The last time I saw you, you tried stabbing me to death!"

"I did?" the chef droid replied. Trying to remember,

K-2PQ reached up with one arm to scratch his metal skull. "So . . . does that mean I'm fired?"

"It seems Olag Greck caused a lot of memory trouble for you all," Boonda laughed. "Now that he's locked up, we can make repairs."

Although Forwun was glad to have his memories restored, he found himself lost in thought. If nothing else, he could not stop thinking about returning to Tatooine one day to destroy EV-9D9.

Watching Boonda and his droids, the Rebels felt relieved to see a happy ending on the planet Vactooine.

"Boonda's droid told quite a story!" Luke Skywalker commented to his friends. "Do you think it's all true?"

"Artoo and I have had some experience with Olag Greck, Master Luke," Threepio stated. "If anyone would have dared to execute such an incredible plan, it would be him!"

"Unlike every other Hutt in the galaxy, Boonda has a funny reputation for telling the truth," Han Solo stated. "Maybe we should ask him to join the Rebellion. What do you think, Princess?"

Gazing at Boonda, Leia declared, "You know my answer to that, Han. The Rebellion can use all the help it can get! Who knows what our next mission will be?"

"Indeed," Boonda laughed. "Indeed."

NEXT MISSION:
PRISONER OF THE NIKTO PIRATES